My Big, New Bed

Crabtree Publishing Company
www.crabtreebooks.com

PMB16A, 350 Fifth Avenue
Suite 3308,
New York, NY

616 Welland Avenue
St. Catharines, ON
L2M 5V6

Published by Crabtree Publishing in 2008

First published in 2007 by
Franklin Watts
(A division of Hachette Children's Books)
338 Euston Road
London   NW1 3BH

Text © Margaret Nash 2007
Illustration © Beccy Blake 2007

The rights of the author and the illustrator of this Work
have been asserted.

Cataloging-in-Publication data is available at the Library of Congress.

ISBN 978-0-7787-3859-6 (rlb)
ISBN 978-0-7787-3890-9 (pbk)

Series Editor: Jackie Hamley
Editor: Melanie Palmer
Series Advisor: Dr Hilary Minns
Series Designer: Peter Scoulding

Printed in the U.S.A.

My Big, New Bed

by Margaret Nash

Illustrated by Beccy Blake

Crabtree Publishing Company

www.crabtreebooks.com

Margaret Nash

"My bed is big and bouncy, and I'm snug as a bug in it. So is my cat, Tabitha, though she sleeps on top of the bed."

Beccy Blake

"Here is a picture of my son Joe bouncing on his big new bed. He loves it. Our cats love it too and spend hours asleep on it."

Dad bought a new bed for me and Ted.

"Let's see how many fit on," I said.

7

My sister came.
She bounced about.

9

My brother came too.
"Yippee!" he cried out.

11

The dog jumped on.
He leapt around.

13

The cat jumped on
in a single bound.

15

We all got tangled up
in the sheet.

17

Soon we heard a very loud CREAK!

19

Then everybody fell
off the bed.

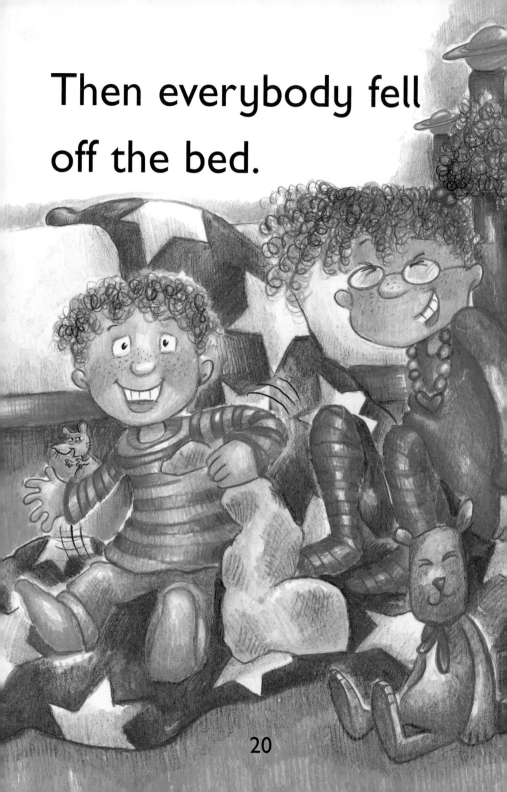

21

"This bed is just for me and Ted."

Notes for adults

TADPOLES are structured to provide support for early readers. The stories may also be used by adults for sharing with young children.

Starting to read alone can be daunting. **TADPOLES** help by providing visual support and repeating high frequency words and phrases. These books will both develop confidence and encourage reading and rereading for pleasure.

If you are reading this book with a child, here are a few suggestions:

1. Make reading fun! Choose a time to read when you and the child are relaxed and have time to share the story.
2. Talk about the story before you start reading. Look at the cover and the blurb. What might the story be about? Why might the child like it?
3. Encourage the child to reread the story, and to retell the story in their own words, using the illustrations to remind them what has happened.
4. Discuss the story and see if the child can relate it to their own experiences, or perhaps compare it to another story they know.
5. Give praise! Children learn best in a positive environment.

If you enjoyed this book, why not try another TADPOLES story?

At the End of the Garden
9780778738503 RLB
9780778738817 PB

Bad Luck, Lucy!
9780778738510 RLB
9780778738824 PB

Ben and the Big Balloon
9780778738602 RLB
9780778738916 PB

Crabby Gabby
9780778738527 RLB
9780778738831 PB

Five Teddy Bears
9780778738534 RLB
9780778738848 PB

I'm Taller Than You!
9780778738541 RLB
9780778738855 PB

Leo's New Pet
9780778738558 RLB
9780778738862 PB

Little Troll
9780778738565 RLB
9780778738879 PB

Mop Top
9780778738572 RLB
9780778738886 PB

My Auntie Susan
9780778738589 RLB
9780778738893 PB

My Big, New Bed
9780778738596 RLB
9780778738909 PB

Pirate Pete
9780778738619 RLB
9780778738923 PB

Runny Honey
9780778738626 RLB
9780778738930 PB

Sammy's Secret
9780778738633 RLB
9780778738947 PB

Sam's Sunflower
9780778738640 RLB
9780778738954 PB